# Olly

## the little white van

# The Bumpton Rally

## A Picture Storybook

Autumn
Publishing

Today is the annual town race in Bumpton. Olly and his driver, Stan, are preparing to take part.

"I'm quite nervous, Stan," Olly admits. "Do you think we can win?"

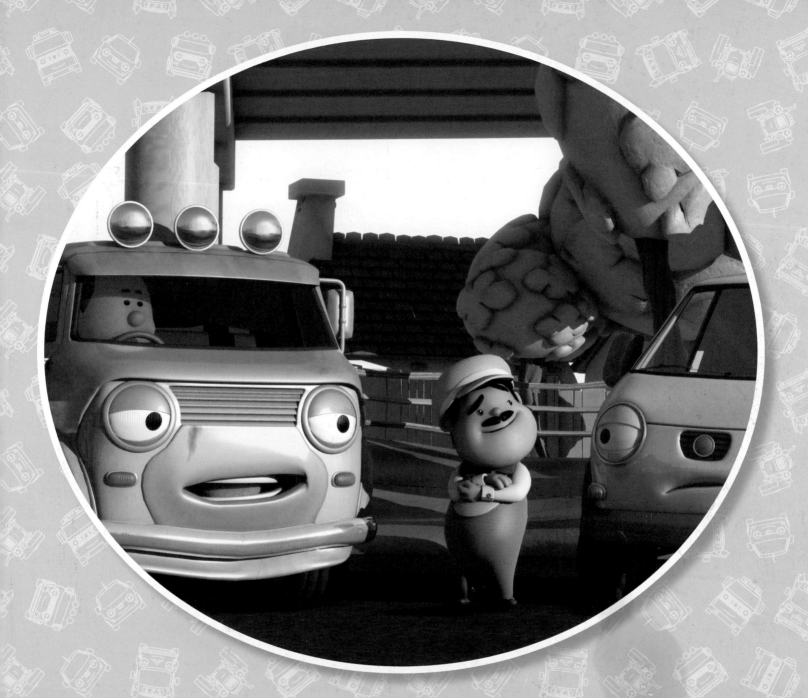

"Not a chance, Olly!" someone shouts from behind. It is Olly's friend, Bazza.

"It's only the annual Bumpton Rally," says Stan, "It's just a bit of fun!"

"It's only fun if you win," replies Bazza.

Bazza is full of confidence. "I will win!" he exclaims with a big grin.
"Are you sure? I'm pretty fast you know," Olly replies.

"You're not as fast as me!" Bazza brags.

A loud call from the race organiser draws their attention.

"Will all vehicles please make their way to the start line."

The racers assemble at the start line. All of them are eager for the rally to begin. But there seems to be someone missing...

To everyone's surprise, Jethro the tractor pulls up at the start line.
"What are you doing here?" Bazza asks. "You're far too slow."
"Speed isn't everything you know!" Jethro says.

"Ready, steady, go!" the speaker announces. The lights flash green and the cars set off with a roar. All except Jethro, who chugs gently off the start line, at his own pace.

The race is on! They drive full speed around the track and past the cheering crowd. The fastest racer, Dirk, is soon in the lead. He is closely followed by Olly.

"How are we doing, Stan?" asks Olly.

"Great, we're in second place!" cheers Stan.

Behind Olly the fight for third place is fierce.

"Move aside, Bazza!" shouts Tasha, trying to overtake him.

"No chance!" Bazza responds, leaving a thick cloud of dust as he speeds off.

Tasha can't see anything through the dust cloud. It causes her to veer off the road, straight into a bush.

Poor Tasha, she's out of the race!

The race is still on! Olly and Bazza race through the countryside. Behind them both, Jethro chugs along slowly.

Bazza is gradually closing in on Olly.
"Get out of the way! Let the winner through!" Bazza shouts.

With all his strength, Olly pushes forward and zooms further ahead.
"See you at the finish line!" Olly laughs.
"Not if I get there first," mutters a grumpy Bazza.

Annoyed that Olly is ahead of him, Bazza decides to take a shortcut. He veers off the road and into a field.

"Where are you going?" Bazza's driver asks worriedly.

But fields are not like roads and they are certainly not meant for driving on! Bazza comes to a sudden halt. He is stuck in a very muddy puddle!

As Olly whizzes down the road, he glimpses an orange figure in the distance. The orange figure is sinking into the mud!

"Who is that?" Olly wonders.

Olly and Stan drive over to see what is going on.

"What happened, Bazza?" questions Olly.

"Olly! Stan! We're sinking!" shouts Bazza, as he slowly disappears into the mud.

Olly, who is always happy to offer a helping hand, jumps into action. He tries to pull Bazza out of the mud. It's not easy as the puddle is very deep. Oh no! Now Olly is stuck, too!

Jethro has finally caught up with them. He sees his friends are in trouble.

"Can I be of some help?" he asks. They are so pleased to see him.

"Better late than never!" laughs Jethro.

The crowd wait anxiously at the finish line, wondering who will cross it. "Here they come!" calls the speaker. "And in second place it's... Jethro!" Jethro is towing Olly and Bazza across the line!

Olly and Stan are so happy they have crossed the finish line, even if they are covered in mud!

"Thank goodness Jethro came to the rescue. He's a great friend!" Olly says with relief.

"He's the best!" agrees Bazza. "He was right, slow and steady does win the race!"

Bazza feels a little silly now. He shouldn't have bragged about being the fastest.

"Well, Bazza, we may not have won the race, but we've certainly won something else," Olly says.

"What's that?" Bazza asks.

"We are the muddiest vans in town!" Olly says, laughing.